UBU IS KING!

A ONE-ACT PLAY

Love,

Mum and Dad x x x

TRANSLATED AND ADAPTED FROM *UBU ROI* BY ALFRED JARRY

BY **CHRISTOPHER CARTER SANDERSON**

tm

UBU IS KING!

A one-act play for street theatre freely adapted from
Ubu Roi by Alfred Jarry

BY
CHRISTOPHER CARTER SANDERSON

UBU IS KING!
Adapted from *Ubu Roi* by Alfred Jarry
BY CHRISTOPHER CARTER SANDERSON

"Set in Poland, a state that at the time had no legal existence, Ubu is an unhistorical burlesque, on the coarsest terms possible, of a history play. Its titular hero, fat, stupid, cowardly, hypocritical, and endlessly greedy, is all human vices rolled into one disgusting package, mirrored by his equally disgusting wife. Through conspiracy, brutality, and betrayal, Ubu conquers Poland, causing uncountable slaughters and miseries, all treated in gross-out comic book terms, before he is overthrown and driven into exile. While Jarry's brief life (d. 1907) barely brushed the 20th century, the figure he had created, appetite incarnate, cast his rotund shadow across the decades of terror to come. As late as the 1990s, directors could picture Ubu harassing the homeless in Grand Central Station or lying to South Africa's Truth Commission. W.B. Yeats, who witnessed the first performance, had been right: Watching Ubu wave the toilet brush that served him as a scepter, the poet thought, 'After us, the savage god.'"

        -- From *Our Theatrical Century*
        by Michael Feingold,
        The Village Voice, December 4, 2000

UBU IS KING!

The road-box is brought to the playing area by the cast. It contains all of the props for the show, and sometimes serves for a level for the action. Drums and music accompany the procession. The music ends as the director introduces the show to the crowd.

Costume note: the actors are all in street clothes, which are white for the most part.
This basic costume is built on very sparely to create the characters. For instance, MA UBU may be created by modifying the posture and facial expression of the actor, and simply adding a fright wig. CAPTAIN MANURE might have an oversized Napoleon hat, etc., except for UBU who is outwardly created by a pointy hat (his head), a half-mask(or pointy nose), and a belt from which is suspended his buttocks and phallus. The phallus must be large and preposterous. Floppy or erect, your choice. When the script indicates TRANSFORMATION, this means a fifteen-second frenetic dance takes place during which UBU is passed to another actor. This ritual punctuates the action, should be accompanied by drums, and result in the ten different actors of the cast all playing UBU for one scene each. The entire ensemble is a part of every scene, even if just framing it; there is no "off-stage" in the street.

"Po' Land" is pronounced as if it is the opposite of "Rich Land." Get it?

"Monophalus" is pronounced and stressed something like "Acropolis" (mon-AW-fuh-lus) and not at all like "Bono Palace."

Special mention is made of the actors who bravely first performed this text in New York City's Grand Central Terminal, in 1990. A mistaken official tossed them and me out unceremoniously due to his mistaken ideas about freedom of speech. Special thanks to the Village Voice, and especially Michael Feingold, and to the ACLU and NYCLU, especially Marjorie Heins, for getting that show back into Grand Central. Special thanks also to all casts of UBU IS KING! since then including those in New York City with Gorilla Rep, the one in Brazil, and the one at The Yale Cabaret.

SCENE ONE

UBU and MA UBU asleep, UBU wakes up. Then he takes a big, runny shit all over the floor. Whoopee cushions sound f/x. In addition, the entire ensemble should proclaim the first line in unison with UBU.

UBU:
Shit!

This wakes MA UBU up and she runs over to toss cat litter, sand, or straw over all the shit on the floor.

MA UBU:
Oh, Ubu, you are a fat, stupid oaf.

UBU:
Shut up, Ma Ubu, or I'll crack your skull.

MA UBU:
You should think of other skulls to bash in,
Ubu, you should think of something better.

UBU:
What the hell are you talking about, Ma?

MA UBU:
Don't tell me you're satisfied with your lot.

UBU:
I am very satisfied with my lot
I've got decorations, I'm a Captain.
The King regards me as a trusted friend.
With my soldiers, I am well respected-

MA UBU:
Respected by fifty starving cripples!
You were once the King in your own kingdom
And you're content to order these poor jerks
When you could be having your head measured
For the crown of all the realm of Po' Land!

7

UBU:
You must have fallen off the bed last night
And bashed your head yourself to think such things.
King Wank is very much alive and has
A load of children if he dies, you fool.

MA UBU:
Kill 'em all and let-

UBU:
                                    I'm gonna kill you!
MA UBU:
Kill me and you won't get your enema.

UBU:
I can do my own enema can't I?

MA UBU:
Forget about your ene*ma* Ubu,
Think about your ene*my* for a change.
If you were king, you could get douched with wine,
You could wipe your ass with the finest silks!
You could roll around in a limousine,
Eat your favorite foods, and shit your favorite-

UBU:
Shits! I could get a crown like my old one,
Which was stolen when the last coup rolled through!

MA UBU:
You could wear anything you wanted to!

UBU:
Oh! If I could get my hands on King Wank-

MA UBU:
Yes! You'll put him in the Wanks of the dead!

UBU:
What am I saying? I am a Captain!
I couldn't murder the King of Po' Land!

8

MA UBU:
Damn! Ubu, do you want to stay poor, then?

UBU:
I'd rather stay poor than listen to you! (*returns to bed*)

MA UBU:
How am I going to be Queen of Po' Land
If I can't get this idiot to act?
Maybe if I invite Captain M'nure,
Ubu will see how easy it would be
To use Manure and his men to work
The killing of the King and make me Queen!
I'll invite M'nure over for supper.

<TRANSFORMATION>

SCENE TWO

OR "UBU, THE INSPIRED"

Later that day.

UBU:
Shut up, Ma Ubu, I'm trying to sleep.

MA UBU:
Get out of bed, you lazy shit, our guests
Will be here any minute. Hurry up!

UBU:
I'm hungry. What have we here? It's chicken!

MA UBU:
Yes, it's chicken, you overstuffed porker.
Leave it be so that our guests can have it.

UBU:
Guests! So that's why you have all that paint
On top of your ugly face. I'm hungry!

MA UBU:
Ubu, none of your asininities,
Now, Captain Manure will be our guest
And he can give you-
                          -hey, not the chicken!
UBU:
By my big flicker, Ma, I've got to eat.

MA UBU:
Here they come-

CAPTAIN MANURE:
Ten-Hut! Cadets sitting down on my mark-
Hut!
Hail, good Ma Ubu, Ubu, hail to you!

MA UBU:
Good day, sir Captain, won't you have some food?
We have Chicken a la King and Cow Pies.
Something for your men-

UBU:
                    -Good God, Ma Ubu!
Don't give them my food, they'll just shit it out!
(Hits them, chases them off)
Now, Manure, how did you like dinner?

MANURE:
Not bad, except for all the shit you slung.

UBU:
Never mind. How would you like a Dukedom?

MANURE:
But, Ubu, you're broke-

UBU:
                    -I will be King soon!

MANURE:
Are you going to kill the King and Queen?

UBU:
Who told you, by my green flick, did you guess?

MANURE:
If you want an able man to help you
In this assassination of the King,
I'll do it, sir, and so will my men.
(a signal to MA UBU)

UBU:
You are like a son to me Manure.

MANURE:
Oh, Ubu, you stink! of this treachery,
But I will help you to become King.
Don't you ever wash your great fat buttocks?

UBU:
Sometimes-

MA UBU:
       -never! He doesn't even wipe!

UBU:
That's all M'nure. I'll send for you later.
And , by all the puss-filled piss-buckets in
Po' Land, I'll make you Duke by next week.

MANURE:
All hail King Ubu!

UBU:
       Quiet now, my pet.

<TRANSFORMATION>

SCENE THREE

OR, "UBU, THE ABJECT"

UBU:
What do you want, man, by my green candle?

MESSENGER:
Ubu, Captain of Dragoons, is summoned
To the presence of His Royal Highness. (*exits*)

UBU:
Oh, no! What's this! The shit has hit the fan,
The King has discovered my treachery!

MA UBU:
Relax, old Ubu, things will be all right.

UBU:
Yes, they will! I'll tell them that you did it!

MA UBU:
If you even try-

UBU:
                    -good-bye, you fat nag.

MA UBU:
Ubu, I'll get you-

UBU:
                    -you'll get a hanging!

MA UBU:
Oh, gods, there he is! (*she hides*)

UBU:
                    -now you'll get what's yours!

MESSENGER:
All hail King Wank, Potentate of Po' Land.

13

UBU:
I confess! I mean I didn't do it!
It wasn't me it was my old woman!
I mean I confess that it wasn't me!
I mean I confess that I am Manure!
I mean, I was Manure, it was him!

KING WANK:
What has happened to-

MANURE:
                              -He's drunk as a dog!

KING WANK:
The poor man seems to have-

MANURE:
                              -I know he's drunk!

MESSENGER:
Three cheers for our King and Benefactor!
Hip, hip-

ALL: Hoo-ray!

MESSENGER: Hip, hip!

ALL: Hoo-ray!

MESSENGER: Hip, hip!

ALL: Hoo-ray!

KING WANK:
            -let it be known that our magnificent
Champion and great Captain of Forces,
Ubu, has pleased us well. And to reward
His faithful, prudent services we will
Create him as our Count of Standolny.

14

UBU:
Thank you! Gracious, fantastic majesty-

KING WANK:
No, no, our once captain now Count Ubu,
We smile on you, and will count on you,
And think of you as our royal tailor;
You shall help us make robes of policy
To cover this, our body politic.
Teach us the fashion of government,
For we feel our current garb outdated.
But, enough of this talk of tailoring.
We'll not keep you on the pins and needles
Of anticipation – come tomorrow,
To our grand review, and be made Count there.

UBU:
How can I repay – (*trips on phallus*) ouch! I'm dying!
Oh, there, I', O.K. I'd hate to think
Of what would happen to Mother Ubu
If I should rupture my monophalus
And die -

KING WANK:
            -we would take good care of her. Now,
We must away to see a brand new play.

UBU:
Won't you have to stand in line, your highness?

KING WANK:
No, no. We shall be given the first row,
We are King, and Wank has its privileges.
Farewell-

UBU:
I will fare well by foul dealing!
And you'll get yours out of that deck of cards.

<TRANSFORMATION>

SCENE FOUR

OR, "UBU THE PLOTTER"

Deep in conference with the plotters.

UBU:
Ah, now good friends we must begin our plots
But, not without remembering our plans.
We'll use our plots and plans to cook a king!
Too many cooks will spoil the recipe
And so we'll start off our session with me.
In the first part, Strangulation to Death
Would do the trick with ropes around the neck.

ALL:
Too long!   -

UBU:
               -alright, we'll think of something else.
In the second part, Starvation to Death
With no food and, therefore none to blame us,
Because by no one's hand will he be killed!

ALL:
Much too long!

UBU:
               -listen, you rabble, shut up!
I bet you don't have any better ones.
Maybe you are right and it won't work out.
I should leave right now and turn you all in.
Then I wouldn't have to worry myself:
You'd be gone and I would be rewarded.

ALL:
No! Down with Ubu! Up with old King Wank!

MA UBU:
You moldy fart-breath! Try it and you'll die.
We'll slice you up and feed you to the dogs!

16

UBU:
That's it! We'll poison the royal hot dogs!

MA UBU:
Shut up, you desiccated old wind bag!

UBU:
Shut up yourself or I'll French-fry your ears.
Listen, we will have election ballots,
And I will run as a New Publican!

ALL:
No way!

MANURE:
            -that party is already full
Of Ubus, sir, you'll have to think again.

UBU:
I've already tried it - what do you think?

MANURE:
How about I split him up the middle,
Jump on him and slice him top-to-toenail?

ALL:
YES!

UBU:
            - alright, I'll take the risks for the job.
When he comes for the review today, I'll
Shuffle up beside him and I'll watch him
Until he looks away and then I'll stomp
On top of his toenails and, when he kicks,
I'll scream out "CHICKENSHIT" and you jump him.
You and all your men should hack him to bits.

ALL:
Yes, Yes!

MANURE:
            -    And then, we'll hack the Princes, all!

ALL:
Yes, Yes, Yes!

MANURE:
 - And then, we'll take the Palace!

ALL:
Yes, Yes, Yes, Yes!

MANURE:
 - And, we'll take the money!

UBU:
Enough, are we agreed on this action?

ALL:
Yes, Yes, Yes, Yes, Yes!

UBU:
But, wait, you must not go before you swear
An oath before your God to do this thing.

MANURE:
But we haven't got a priest to do it.

UBU:
I will be Church and State, so swear to me.

ALL:
Hail, Ubu!

UBU:
 - Do you swear to snag King Wank?

ALL:
Holy Ubu!

UBU:
 - Do you swear to kill him?

ALL:
We swear! All hail Ubu, Ubu is King! <TRANSFORMATION>

SCENE FIVE

OR, "UBU THE USURPER"

QUEEN ROSEBUD:
You'll die! You'll die! I know, my noble King
I saw that Ubu in a dream last night
Descending like a suffocating fog
Or perhaps a cloud of putrefying fart-gas
To strangle and destroy your kingly self.
I dreamed I saw him take the crown from you
And put it on his big, fat, stupid head.

KING WANK:
Whose head did you say, my gentle Rosebud?

QUEEN ROSEBUD:
Ubu, the man you want to make a Count!

KING WANK:
Nonsense. I will trust Ubu completely.
And, you will not attend the Grand Review-
Think instead about these lies you're spreading
And learn to think of Ubu as friend.

QUEEN ROSEBUD:
I hope that you don't learn a lesson grave
And costly to your country. God save you! (*she exits*)

KING WANK:
Greetings, Captain Ubu, stand beside me.
I now proclaim you Count. Start the parade!
What fine marching troops we have, Count Ubu.

UBU:
Fine if you don't see the rust on their swords,
Their athlete's foot, their jock-itch and shin-splints.
They look as stupid as their shitty King!

KING WANK:
What happened to your manners, Count Ubu?

UBU:
They seem to have turned into CHICKENSHIT!

SOLDIERS:
Yah!

(During the battle choreography, as they kill the King:)

UBU:
Chop and hack your way to the top, raiders,
Take what you deserve! You deserve the best!
The best is expensive, but you're worth it !
Don't ask questions, Just Do It! Just Do It!
Just kill 'em all and let God sort 'em out!
We'll build a memorial later on!
We'll send economic aid to their graves!

KING WANK:
Oh, Holy Virgin, I'm dying, I'm dead!

UBU:
Here is the crown, now I will put it on.
Now, dummy up and listen to my speech
On the People's Science of Pataphysics.
It's based on simple metabolic facts.
The world is made up of two kinds of things:
Shit and Cash. If you're alive, then you're Cash
And if you've died, then you become Shit.
I will be your Master of Phynances
And sort out those of you who have the Cash
From those of you who I will turn to Shit.

SOLDIERS:
Hail King Ubu, Master of Phynances!

MANURE:
And now, King Ubu, you must share the spoils!

UBU:
Share, my ass, you want to take my goodies!

MANURE:
You can keep your ass, just give us some loot.

20

UBU:
Loot yourselves! I'll put you in the stew pot!

MA UBU:
What the hell's the matter with you, Ubu?
You've got everything you want haven't you?
Come on! Government is like your bowels,
If you don't give something back, you'll burst!
You're the one that will end up in the stew.
Just give them a little incentives-

UBU:
But I'm King now!

MA UBU:
                      - Just give them a little!
And give them forms to fill out to get it,
They'll have to wait while the paper's printed,
And more than half of them can't even write.
Those that can will be stuck filling out forms -
All in triplicate - and they'll make mistakes.
By the time it's all over, nothing's paid!
You win, but you seem to be generous.
The people will take you into their hearts.
Meanwhile, they'll forget about their pockets!

UBU:
But, taxes are supposed to be paid!

MANURE:
If you do not give the troops some money,
How will they be able to pay your taxes?
They won't pay your taxes if you stiff them.

UBU:
In that case, I will throw a feast for them!
And an Orgy and a Raucous Vict'ry Dance!

SOLDIERS: *(old-fashioned conga line beat)*
Oo, Ah, Oh-Yeah! Oo, Ah, Oh-Yeah! Oo, Ah...

<TRANSFORMATION *during dance*>

SCENE SIX

OR, "UBU THE VILE"

Alone with the Queen.

UBU:
And, now, Queen Rosebud, your old king is dead,
He's gone to feed the worms under the ground.
One day I might eat the fish that ate the
Worms that ate your king, and shit it back out.
And, thus, you might be married to my shits!
And so *we're* almost married already!
Be my concubine and I will spare you.

QUEEN ROSEBUD:
Set down your ass upon that ground, Ubu,
And beg forgiveness of my royal self.
I reject your evil, stinking offers
And condemn your spirit to the hell fires!
May you burn a thousand ears for ev'ry
Ounce of fat upon your wicked body!
Death will dine on you, and I will help it!

UBU:
Not so fast, lady-

MA UBU;
                    - What are you doing? (*Ubu is distracted and the Queen runs away*)

UBU:
Shut your mouth and address me as King!

MA UBU:
You are a king-sized idiot, Ubu!
And you won't be that for long, now,
If you let Queen Rosebud escape from here.

UBU:
Nonsense, she's right here-

MA UBU:

                       - she's where , you cowflop?

UBU:

She was here until you came and farted,
And distracted the Master of Phynance
From his duties as the Royal Phucker,
Queen Rosebud who I hoped to bed has fled.
I will be forced to try a Flying Fuck!

MA UBU:

Ubu, have you been pinching the wineskins?
You're not making any sense, you fat dope.
Go and catch the Queen before she escapes!

UBU:

By my big green dick, I'm too stuffed to run,
It was all I could do last night to keep
My belly from exploding, Ma Ubu.

MA UBU:

She'll explode your belly for you, Ubu,
If you don't track her down and kill her now.
She will return and try to take the throne.

UBU:

Ridiculous, you old fat sow, shut up!
I've got better things to do than run
To catch someone who's not even Queen now.
My head is feeling cold -

MA UBU:

                     - Oo, Pa Ubu!

UBU:

I mean my royal noggin, you sausage.
I have ordered myself a great hat made,
Big enough to top my king-sized head with.

MA UBU:

You've got to be frugal with money,
Pig-nosed loon, or we'll lose it all too soon.
What's this bonnet made of, Mister Ubu?

23

UBU:
It's a big tall hat-

MA UBU:
                    - how much did you waste?

UBU:
Made of cheep sheepskin, and it has ribbons
And little buckles-

MA UBU:
                    - how much did they cost?

UBU:
They're made of doghide!

MA UBU(+ALL):
                    - you killed animals?!

UBU:
Just one stupid dog!

MA UBU:
                        - Well, it sounds O.K.
But being royalty couple is best.

UBU:
Yes, but there are many nobles left, still
And don't they each have some small royalty?
If we kill them all and take their titles
We can take their royalties and have more!
And I will take all of their cash as well!

<TRANSFORMATION>

SCENE SEVEN

OR, "UBU, THE KING"

UBU:
Of all the nobles, I am the noblest,
And therefore my science is highest!
Pataphysics - pride of Philosophy.
Observe: that which is not mine soon will be
And, thereupon, it was mine all along!
The Gravitational Corollary
Being postulated that as I grow
Fatter my Gravity increases thus
And I attract more, which is attracted
By my Fat and is Therefore also mine!
Of course, the Political Aspects are
That I am King and Master of Phynance
In charge of all the monies of the land
Which I now command to return to me.
Tax, Tariff and Surcharge Universal
Charged to everyone, retroactively!

MA UBU:
What will be left, fool?

UBU:
                        - My list of titles.
Shut up! I have Matters of State to find.
It matters that I find the nobles' cash.
Bring in the nobles!

MANURE:
                        - Yes, Sir! King Ubu!

UBU:
What is your name, man -?

NOBLE #1:
                        - Duke of Cumberland.

UBU:
What is your income?

NOBLE #1:
                    - A million dollars.

UBU:
Throw him to the disembraining machine!
One million bucks a noble! Throw them all!

MA UBU:
You are being too bloodthirsty, Ubu.

UBU:
Madame my bitch I am a maestro,
Conducting all the Cash into my hands.
Be quiet and tell me about the judges.

MA UBU:
The Court is full, you cannot appoint -

UBU:
I'll appoint a new court, I'll be the Court.
I'll set precedence that gives me the Cash!
Read me my list of noble titles now.

MANURE:
Count of the Sea Port -

UBU:
                    -Start with the Princedoms!

MANURE:
Grand Prince of Central, Prince of Nolia,
Potentate of Prydania, Prince of -

UBU:
That's enough, the rest are irrelevant!
It's time to take taxes from the people.
They're the only ones left with any cash.
Soldiers, spread out and take donations now!

(the soldiers pan-handle the crowd)

This taxation is tax deductible,
My kingdom is **by** the people's wallets'
For the people who pay generously,
And **of** the pockets of the other ones.

MANURE:
Ubu, this is mad.

UBU:

                        - Don't be a traitor!
It's time to raise our taxes and Cash In.

<TRANSFORMATION>

SCENE EIGHT

OR, "UBU, THE COMMANDER"

UBU:
I hereby call this meeting to order.
Desport thyselves, Phynancial Gentlemen.
Ah, yes, we must discourse on Phynasses-

MA UBU:
You're a fat fine-ass yourself, old Ubu.

UBU:
Shut up, or I'll grill you good and proper!
As We were saying, our Phynass is fat.
Everywhere you look, you can see it blossom -
Fine huge explosions destroy the buildings
Like great roaring orange dandelions
Springing up in fields of dust and wreckage.
The arms of the starving wave like poppies-
Waving in the wind of Our Phynass!
Everywhere the music of destruction!
We have decreed a royal ban on rain,
So that the Fires of Our Phynass may burn!

MA UBU:
Sounds like hemorrhoids -

COUNSELOR:
                              - splendid Your Highness!

MA UBU:
No, His Hemorrhoids are on His Anus!

UBU:
Madame of Our Phynance, silence yourself!

COUNSELOR:
Your taxes, Sire, how go your new taxes?

UBU:
Not as well as they may have, I'm afraid.

MA UBU:
His marriage tax has been complete bust.

UBU:
I've tried to force people to get married -
These people just don't have the Right Values!

MA UBU:
And, his tax on dying hasn't worked out.

UBU:
But, I've been killing people Left and Right!

MANURE:
So, of course, there's no one left to tax now.
Why don't you give me that Dukedom King Ubu?
I've put you in power and earned it well.

UBU:
Traitor! Phynancial Soldiers, arrest him!
Throw him in the lowest dungeon there is!

MANURE:
I swear vengeance on you, Ubu, you pig.
I will restore the rightful Queen or die!

UBU:
Well first you can dance a jig with the rats!
Hold him down well, Phynancial Paladins!
Now, as We were saying, about dinner -

SOLDIERS:
WHERE?!

UBU:
You've let him escape! Ouch ! He's clouted me!

MANURE:
I run now, Ubu, but I shall return!
I will restore Queen or die trying!

UBU:
Oh, let him go. We have other problems.
Like how to convince the people to pay.

MA UBU:
Manure will bring the Russian Army
To restore Queen Rosebud to her title.
You had better prepare your armies, too!

COUNSELOR:
Yes, of course! War will convince the people!
They will pay the price to see a good war on!

UBU:
Victory's within our reach, dear friends, our reach!
Or, close enough for it to be there soon-
Phynancial Paladins, prepare to fight.
In peace, I know, there's nothing quite as nice
As modest taxing and plain extortion,
But, when the drum of war bangs in our ears,
We've got to get angry and excited -
Be terrible Tigers of Taxation!
Now, crunch your teeth and stretch your nostrils wide!
If you're scared, some drink will give you courage,
Some spirit! On, on, noblest Paladins,
And collect the taxes for the war.
Now we hereby declare a special tax
On the bullets and the bombs of war
Remember to tax every bullet shot!
Just think of them all lined up and ready
Chomping at the bit like little greyhounds.
Bring my financial Horse of War,
Vict'ry's within our reach, dear friends, our reach!

<TRANSFORMATION>

SCENE NINE

OR, "UBU THE WARLORD"

Ubu is now on stilts, with a cardboard horse. He walks around the audience during Ma Ubu's little scene saying variations of this line:

UBU:
Woah! Easy, my fine Phynancial Charger !

MA UBU:
At least that fat oaf is out of the way.
I've heard that the old king's treasure is here
Among the tombs of the Kings of Po' Land.
Let's see - One, Two, Three, Four, Five, Six, Seven.
Here's the treasure of the Kings in Heaven.
This should be the tomb that has the treasures.
Oh, that must be it rattling around,
The gold must be mixed up with all the bones.

GHOST:
Oh-hh-hh-hh-hh! Never, Ma Ubu!

MA UBU:
Ah-hh-hh-hh-hh! You can keep th'shit!

(she runs off)

UBU:
Line up now, you Warlike Tax Collectors,
You Phynancial Soldiers, do your duty.
We are tired from marching and will rest here.
Sound off your numbers-

SOLDIERS:
                              - One! Two! Three! Four! Sir!

UBU:
Well, we've marched and marched and there's no Russians!
What do you suppose -

31

MANURE:
(leaping up)

                        - Ah-Ha, It's Ubu!
Surrender, we have taken the palace,
Ma Ubu has abandoned it to us,
And Queen Rosebud sits upon the throne now!
Lay down your weapons or we will kill you!

QUEEN ROSEBUD:
We declare all of your taxes over!

MANURE:
Charge! Down with the tyranny of Ubu!

(there is a great scuffle)

UBU:
Tax them triplicate! Demand Payment!
Now, Manure, I will kill you myself!
Oh, no! I've been hit! Oh, God, a cannon!

MANURE:
That was just your charger farting, Ubu.

UBU:
Damn your insolence! Take that, you traitor!

SOLDIER:
He's killed Manure, our old Captain!

ANOTHER SOLDIER:
No more taxes and killing! Fight Ubu! *(they all turn on him)*

UBU:
So that's how it's going to be, you shits!
Well, I'll peel you with my shit-kicker
And Kick you with my Phynancial Peeler.
Do your duty, Sword of my Pynances!
Slice them like a pie chart, Phynancial Sword!
Do your best to help it on its way now,
My fine Phynancial Charger! Shit on them!

SOLDIERS:
Down with Ubu! Down with Ubu! Kill him!

UBU:
Ouch! Stop poking me, you bunch of stinking dogs!
Run, Phynancial Charger- let's get away!
I'm tired of all this governmental stuff,
There's only one thing left to save us,
Shut your eyes and run, my good horse!

<TRANSFORMATION>

SCENE TEN

OR, "UBU THE EXILE"

UBU AND MA UBU:
(in a cave, they speak simultaneously, and they don't see each other)
I'm finally alone, and that is fine.
It feels like I've been running for eight YEARS
across that endless snow-covered desert.
Everything seems to have gone wrong at once!

MA UBU:
(Ubu sits down and Ma advances, still not seeing him)
Right after Ubu ran off on his horse,
I tried to grab the treasure from the crypt
And before I dared to try it again,
I was nearly stoned to death by M'nure.
He rallied what was left of the nobles,
And they ran me away from the Palace.
I jumped the wall and swam across the moat
But they still pursued me like rabid dogs!
(Ubu falls asleep, MA:)
I finally managed to escape the mob
And hiked across the snow to find this cave.

UBU:
(In his sleep)
Somebody catch Ma Ubu and roast her!

MA UBU:
Oh!

UBU:
Tie her up tightly and toast her!

MA UBU:
Hey! It's that fat oaf! It seems he's sleeping.

UBU:
List, list, oh read me my list of titles.
Make somebody take the teddy-bears' knives!

34

Stop them from sticking me, I'll tax their fur.
Oh, Ma Ubu, I'm going to roast you!
Killing, and Perforating, and Taxing!
Oh, Queen Rosebud, I want you to marry me!
Killing and taxing are my only joys!

MA UBU:
That fat jerk was trying to boink the Queen!
Well, I'll get even with him, the toad-butt.

UBU:
(he wakes up, but Ma Ubu puts her hands over his eyes)
It's very dark inside this awful cave.

MA UBU:
(she growls) Grrr!

UBU:
Oh, my God it's a big bear! Help me! Oh!

MA UBU:
Ubu, I'm your guardian Angel,
Shut up and listen to my good advice.
You should be humble, you great, fat asshole!

UBU:
Hey, Angels aren't supposed to curse like that!

MA UBU:
Quiet! And be afraid for all your sins!
Now, don't you have a wife, you old sinner?

UBU:
Yes, she's that died up old hag called Ma Ubu.

MA UBU:
You must forgive her to become holy!

UBU:
Forgive her for what?

MA UBU:

                    - stealing a little.

UBU:
She pocketed my Cash?! That's good to know.

MA UBU:
She just took a little pocket money -

UBU:
Hey! It's you, you ridiculous hag-witch!
Don't try to pull one over on Ubu!

MA UBU:
Easy, Ubu, I'm your only friend left.

UBU:
Nonsense! Now, bend over for your spanking!

MA UBU:
Stop it, Ubu -

UBU:

                - Give me one good reason!

MA UBU:
Ubu, you should think of something better!

UBU:
What the hell are you talking about, Ma?

MA UBU:
We should get ourselves a nicer place!
Let's find ourselves a ship and sail away.

UBU:
The best idea you've ever had!
I'm glad I thought of it, let's sail away!
Ho, there, Mister Captain, hoist the sail up!
Mister Ship Captain, I'll make you a Duke!

The mast and spars of the ship rise all around them. The voices of the crew readying the ship are heard. All other props are loaded into the box and, when the ship sails, all of the bags and baggage, instruments and props, are brought away as part of the ship.

MA UBU:
What country are we sailing to, Ubu?

UBU:
A brand-new island for our phynance, dear.
Let's follow the *Fairy to Manhattan!

MA UBU:
Is there anything left of it, Ubu?

UBU:
Of course there is- Hoist the sail! Weigh anchor!-
Because, if there wasn't any *New York
Left -

ALL:
(as they wave goodbye and the ship sails on,)
        - THERE WOULDN'T BE ANY *NEW YORKERS!

Ma Ubu starts singing.

*These lines can be altered to mention the location of the current production.

The End

nytheatre.com review by Martin Denton reprinted by permission:

UBU IS KING!

How do you make something that was outrageously and outlandishly objectionable and obscene a hundred years ago into something similarly provocative today? Christopher Carter Sanderson and his Gorilla Repertory Theatre have found an entirely successful solution with their production Ubu is King!, which re-imagines Alfred Jarry's early surrealist satire as a thoroughly contemporary romp in the park. I mean this literally, by the way: Ubu is performed in Washington Square Park, one of Gorilla's traditional stamping grounds. And as played by ten high-energy and high-spirited actors, watched over by director Sanderson (himself on the drums), the emphasis is entirely on having fun.

Sanderson's approach to Ubu is, I think, the best possible one. Jarry's play, with its repeated "merdes" and deliberately offensive dialogue and plotting, nevertheless barely registers as mildly naughty in this a world where *There's Something About Mary* is considered mainstream comedy. Wrapping Ubu up in a free-wheeling commedia dell'arte sensibility, complete with a road-box containing props and masks and a giant phallus and buttocks for the actor playing Ubu, is grandly satisfying. And if some of the play's satirical jabs still manage to draw a little blood, well, so much the better.

The best of Sanderson's staging ideas is to have a different actor play Ubu in each of the plays ten scenes. This allows all ten of the players to get his or her moment in the spotlight, and they all rise to the occasion with alacrity. (It also means that everyone gets a crack at shrewish Mama Ubu, as well as various other characters such as Captain Manure and King Wank.) My favorite Ubus were Andre-Phillippe Mistier and disarmingly petite Aedin Moloney; and I loved David Blasher's Manure, so to speak.

The plot, by the way, revolves around Ubu's plan to murder King Wank and seize the crown of Poland for himself. Ubu turns out to be such a vile and tyrannical king that everyone eventually turns against him, and the play ends with Ubu heading off to a distant island to start over. (Guess which island.) The story serves principally as occasion for broad comedy of all sorts, ranging from foolish slapstick to scatological humor to inevitable puns like the King's declaration that "Wank has its privileges." Trust me: the audience is having such a good time that no one bothers to groan.

Ubu is King! plays only one more week this summer, and it's free. Head on down to the park and take it in.

(reviewed July 14, 2000)

Although there have been many productions of UBU IS KING! Presented by Gorilla Rep NYC (www.gorillarep.org) and others since it was written in 1991, this edition is the script prepared for Gorilla Rep's production in Washington Square Park, NYC, July 2000. The cast of that production was as follows:

In Scene One Ubu The Captain was played by Josie Whittlesey, Ma Ubu was played by Eric Dean Scott.

In Scene Two Ubu The Inspired was played by Reggie Austin, Ma Ubu was played by David Blasher, Captain Manure was played by Andre-Philippe Mistier, The Chicken was played by Eric Dean Scott, and the the rest of the ensemble played Manure's men.

In Scene Three Ubu The Abject was played by Eric Dean Scott, Messenger was played by Rachel Jackson, Ma Ubu was played by Aedin Maloney, King Wank by David Blasher, Captain Manure by Matt Freeman, and the marching troops by the rest of the ensemble.

Scene Four Ubu The Plotter was played by Andre-Philippe Mistier.

Scene Five Ubu The Usurper was played by Adria Lang.

Scene Six Ubu The Vile was played by Aedin Maloney.

Scene Seven Ubu The King was played by Tracy Appleton.

Scene Eight Ubu The Commander was played by Matt Freeman.

Scene Nine Ubu The Warlord was played by Rachel Jackson.

Scene Ten Ubu The Exile was played by David Blasher.

UBU IS KING!

Adapted from *Ubu Roi* by Alfred Jarry

BY CHRISTOPHER CARTER SANDERSON

"…Artistic Director Christopher Carter Sanderson has spent a decade building a reputation as one of the finest directors of outdoor and environmental Shakespeare since Joseph Papp…"

- Leonard Jacobs, **theatermania.com**

"… Sanderson's approach to Ubu is, I think, the best possible one… grandly satisfying … And if some of the play's satirical jabs still manage to draw a little blood, well, so much the better…"

- Martin Denton, **nytheatre.com**

Since its premier just before the turn of the last century, Alfred Jarry's *Ubu Roi* has been causing controversy. Students and fans of the theater know of its importance, and the importance of producing it again and again. And yet, the original five-act script can be cumbersome and the irreverent tone of the original French difficult to capture. Here, noted director Christopher Carter Sanderson, founding artistic director of Gorilla Rep NYC brings us a manageable one-act version with all of the sting and punch of the original intact, translated and adapted for contemporary audiences. Over a decade of celebrated productions have tested the veracity of UBU IS KING! which has proved to be as controversial and vital as Alfred Jarry's.

Christopher Carter Sanderson is also the author of *Gorilla Theatre* (Routledge 2003), has served on the faculties of Princeton and Yale Universities, and has directed over 60 productions in New York City.

Printed in Great Britain
by Amazon.co.uk, Ltd.,
Marston Gate.